A Tremendous Wh
Eagles vs Sharks

Hello sports fans! Everyone is on the edge of their seat as this championship baseball game is going into the ninth inning. Will the Eagles or the Sharks win the game? Wow, we are in for an exciting finish as both teams are playing well. The players are ready as the game is set to resume, so let's check out the action between the Eagles and Sharks.

ISBN 978-0-9808866-0-3

Practice early reading skills using the special page format.
- see our Literacy Guide on page 54 -

Support the literacy development of all children.
www.boysRreading.com

ColorSports Publishing Inc.

ColorSports Publishing Inc. - 5 Livingstone Dr. - Dundas - L9H 7S3 - Ontario - Canada

Printed in China

Welcome baseball fans, kids, parents, grammas and gramps.
Who will win this big game and be this year's new champs?

Will it be the Eagles? They throw and catch the ball with such precision.
And when at bat, the red, white and blue can hit with their great vision.

But the Sharks will get on base to score runs and dominate the play.
The white, yellow and red will strike you out, to eliminate their prey.

What tension, with the score 4 to 3 for the Sharks, they are winning.
Let's get to the action as the Sharks are at bat in the 9th inning.

A a
B b
C c
D d
E e
F f
G g
H h
I i
J j
K k
L l
M m
N n
O o
P p
Q q
R r
S s
T t
U u
V v
W w
X x
Y y
Z z

The Eagle fielders are ready to play defense and get three outs.

fielders

ready

play

defense

three

outs

batter

runner

set

let's

play

ball

umpire

shouts

The Shark batter and runner are set,
"Let's play ball," the umpire shouts.

A a
B b
C c
D d
E e
F f
G g
H h
I i
J j
K k
L l
M m
N n
O o
P p
Q q
R r
S s
T t
U u
V v
W w
X x
Y y
Z z

The pitcher checks the runner
as he goes into his wind up.

pitcher

checks

runner

goes

into

wind

up

base

waits

go

time

make

mind

up

©C.HICKS/96

The base runner waits. Will he go?
It's time to make his mind up.

A a
B b
C c
D d
E e
F f
G g
H h
I i
J j
K k
L l
M m
N n
O o
P p
Q q
R r
S s
T t
U u
V v
W w
X x
Y y
Z z

There he goes! As the pitcher turns the runner takes off with great speed.

6

pitcher

turns

runner

takes

off

great

speed

steps

pitch

quickly

knowing

took

good

lead

The Eagle steps to throw his pitch
knowing the Shark took a good lead.

A swing and a miss! All at once the catcher stands to make a throw.

swing

miss

catcher

stands

at

once

make

throw

aims

second

baseman

shark

runner

go

He aims for his second baseman
as he sees the Shark runner go.

A   a
B   b
C   c
D   d
E   e
F   f
G   g
H   h
I   i
J   j
K   k
L   l
M   m
N   n
O   o
P   p
Q   q
R   r
S   s
T   t
U   u
V   v
W   w
X   x
Y   y
Z   z

The runner tries to steal second base, he runs and slides for the bag.

runner

tries

steal

second

base

slides

bag

umpire

shouts

OUT!

Eagle

grabs

puts

tag

The umpire calls, "OUT!" The Eagle grabs the ball and puts on the tag.

A a
B b
C c
D d
E e
F f
G g
H h
I i
J j
K k
L l
M m
N n
O o
P p
Q q
R r
S s
T t
U u
V v
W w
X x
Y y
Z z

With 1-out, the next pitch flies in and the batter likes it.

with
out
next
pitch
flies
batter
likes
Pop!
Shark
ball
swings
bat
strikes
it

"Pop!" goes the ball, as the Shark
swings his bat and strikes it.

©C.HICKS/96

It's a hit past the infield, as the
Shark takes off with a quick burst.

past

infield

batter

takes

off

quick

burst

He's

base

before

throw-in

ump

safe

first

He's at the base before the throw-in
so the ump calls, "Safe at first!"

A a
B b
C c
D d
E e
F f
G g
H h
I i
J j
K k
L l
M m
N n
O o
P p
Q q
R r
S s
T t
U u
V v
W w
X x
Y y
Z z

©C.HICKS/96

In comes the pitch as the Shark
sprints for second base and hustles.

comes

pitch

Shark

sprints

second

base

hustles

batter

swings

hard

fast

ball

with

muscles

The Shark batter swings hard and
fast at the ball with his muscles.

A	a
B	b
C	c
D	d
E	e
F	f
G	g
H	h
I	i
J	j
K	k
L	l
M	m
N	n
O	o
P	p
Q	q
R	r
S	s
T	t
U	u
V	v
W	w
X	x
Y	y
Z	z

The Eagle shortstop scoops up
the ball and then whips it across.

Eagle shortstop scoops up ball whips across second baseman foot bag snags quick toss

With his foot on the bag the second baseman snags the quick toss.

A a
B b
C c
D d
E e
F f
G g
H h
I i
J j
K k
L l
M m
N n
O o
P p
Q q
R r
S s
T t
U u
V v
W w
X x
Y y
Z z

The Shark slides as the Eagle
baseman jumps up to avoid a crash.

Shark

slides

Eagle

baseman

jumps

avoid

crash

OUT

ump

fires

ball

first

quick

flash

"OUT!" calls the ump. He fires
the ball to first, as quick as a flash.

A a
B b
C c
D d
E e
F f
G g
H h
I i
J j
K k
L l
M m
N n
O o
P p
Q q
R r
S s
T t
U u
V v
W w
X x
Y y
Z z

The Shark sprints as the Eagle grabs the ball, to complete the relay.

sprints

first

grabs

ball

complete

relay

umpire

makes

call

OUT

first

base

double

play

The umpire makes the call, "*OUT at first base*," to make a double play.

The Eagles come to bat as the
Shark pitcher flings a fast one.

NINTH INNING VICTORY

EXCITING PLAY-BY-P

Eagles

come

bat

Shark

pitcher

flings

fast

one

batter

turns

quickly

swings

home

run

©C.HICKS/96

The Eagle batter turns quickly
and swings for a home run.

A a
B b
C c
D d
E e
F f
G g
H h
I i
J j
K k
L l
M m
N n
O o
P p
Q q
R r
S s
T t
U u
V v
W w
X x
Y y
Z z

©C.D.HICKS/96

Oh! It's a well hit ball, soaring high to the out-field and deep.

Oh!

well

hit

ball

soaring

high

out-field

deep

Shark

races

wall

catches

big

leap

The Shark races to the wall and catches it with a big leap.

A a
B b
C c
D d
E e
F f
G g
H h
I i
J j
K k
L l
M m
N n
O o
P p
Q q
R r
S s
T t
U u
V v
W w
X x
Y y
Z z

© C. HICKS/96

The next pitch is a curve ball, he fires and aims for his catcher's mitt.

next

pitch

curve

fires

aims

catcher's

mitt

ball

off

bat

swings

through

good

hit

The ball flies off the Eagle's bat as he swings through, getting a good hit.

A a
B b
C c
D d
E e
F f
G g
H h
I i
J j
K k
L l
M m
N n
O o
P p
Q q
R r
S s
T t
U u
V v
W w
X x
Y y
Z z

He runs all the way to second base,
giving the Sharks a little trouble.

runs

all

way

second

giving

little

trouble

fielder

whips

ball

hold

him

stop

double

©C.HICKS/96

The fielder whips the ball in, to hold him and stop him at a double.

A a
B b
C c
D d
E e
F f
G g
H h
I i
J j
K k
L l
M m
N n
O o
P p
Q q
R r
S s
T t
U u
V v
W w
X x
Y y
Z z

The Shark pitcher whips in a hot
fast ball, he brings in the heat.

pitcher

whips

hot

fast

ball

brings

heat

runner

goes

batter

swings

quick

digs

cleat

The runner goes as the batter
swings quick and digs in his cleat.

33

A a
B b
C c
D d
E e
F f
G g
H h
I i
J j
K k
L l
M m
N n
O o
P p
Q q
R r
S s
T t
U u
V v
W w
X x
Y y
Z z

©C.HICKS/96

The ball rockets past the pitcher
as he steps forward off his mound.

34

ball

rockets

past

pitcher

steps

forward

mound

Shark

shortstop

dives

ball

bounces

off

ground

The Shark shortstop dives for the ball as it bounces off the ground.

A a
B b
C c
D d
E e
F f
G g
H h
I i
J j
K k
L l
M m
N n
O o
P p
Q q
R r
S s
T t
U u
V v
W w
X x
Y y
Z z

© C. HICKS/96

The runner races fast for home as the Shark catcher waits at the plate.

runner

races

home

catcher

waits

plate

Safe!

tie

game

ball

tag

come

too

late

He's Safe! The Eagles tie the game as
the ball and the tag come too late.

A	a
B	b
C	c
D	d
E	e
F	f
G	g
H	h
I	i
J	j
K	k
L	l
M	m
N	n
O	o
P	p
Q	q
R	r
S	s
T	t
U	u
V	v
W	w
X	x
Y	y
Z	z

What *pressure*! The next run wins! This batter waits with great anticipation.

pressure

next

run

wins

batter

waits

great

anticipation

pitcher

whips

curve

ball

daring

determination

The Shark pitcher whips in his curve ball with daring determination.

A a
B b
C c
D d
E e
F f
G g
H h
I i
J j
K k
L l
M m
N n
O o
P p
Q q
R r
S s
T t
U u
V v
W w
X x
Y y
Z z

The Eagle swings fast and the fans jump up to a thunderous crack.

Eagle

swings

hard

fans

jump

thunderous

crack

bat

meets

ball

crushes

with

tremendous

whack

His bat meets the ball and crushes
it hard with a tremendous whack.

A a
B b
C c
D d
E e
F f
G g
H h
I i
J j
K k
L l
M m
N n
O o
P p
Q q
R r
S s
T t
U u
V v
W w
X x
Y y
Z z

The ball flies to the wall as the Shark batter swings with all of his might.

ball

flies

wall

Shark

batter

swings

might

catcher

frozen

everyone

turns

watch

ball's

flight

The catcher seems frozen as everyone turns to watch the ball's flight.

A a
B b
C c
D d
E e
F f
G g
H h
I i
J j
K k
L l
M m
N n
O o
P p
Q q
R r
S s
T t
U u
V v
W w
X x
Y y
Z z

©C.HICKS/96

A Shark jumps and stretches for the ball, to stop a game winning run.

jumps

stretches

ball

stop

game

winning

run

sails

past

glove

reach

ninth

inning

done

But it sails past his glove, out of
reach and the ninth inning is done.

45

A a
B b
C c
D d
E e
F f
G g
H h
I i
J j
K k
L l
M m
N n
O o
P p
Q q
R r
S s
T t
U u
V v
W w
X x
Y y
Z z

©C.HICKS/96

Oh baby! It's gone! A home run!
He runs and rounds all the bases.

Oh gone home run runs rounds bases Eagles win Sharks tried hard stand frowns faces

The Eagles win! The Sharks tried hard but stand with frowns on their faces.

Wow! What fun and excitement for the fans who came.
The Sharks and Eagles played an awesome game.

The players fought hard with no energy to spare.
In the heat of the battle they always played fair.

The players now walk about and greet one another.
They reach to shake hands showing respect for each other.

Yes, winning the championship is a sensation.
And playing with sportsmanship wins admiration.

Baseball Player Positions

Offensive Players: When a team has its turn at bat all of their players become offensive players, each player becomes a hitter getting a turn at bat. Each batter stands in the batter's box and tries to get on base by hitting the baseball when it is pitched to them.

Defensive Players: When a team is not at bat nine players make up the defensive team. Each player plays a specific position and has an important role in helping to get outs and to prevent the other team from scoring runs. The nine players are pitcher, catcher, first base, second base, shortstop, third base, right field, center field, and left field.

Pitcher: The player who pitches the ball to each batter, by throwing the ball over or near home plate to the catcher. He plays his position from the pitching mound in the center of the baseball infield. Pitchers will try to throw strikes and also try to throw the baseball to the catcher in different locations to make the batter swing and miss the ball. They will throw fast balls, curve balls and change the speed of the ball to try and fool the batter with each pitch. Pitchers also play defense around the mound when a baseball is hit.

Catcher: The defensive player whose position is directly behind home plate. He catches each pitch thrown by the pitcher. The catcher gives the pitcher a target with his glove and will give signals to the pitcher on where to pitch the ball and what kind of pitch to throw. Catchers also play defense around home plate when the ball is hit.

First Baseman: The player who plays near first base. He is responsible for making an out by touching first base after he catches the ball before an opposing runner tries to touch first base. They also play defense around first base when the ball is hit.

Second Baseman: The player who plays near second base. He is responsible for making an out by touching second base after he catches the ball before an opposing runner tries to touch second base. They also play defense around second base when the ball is hit.

Third Baseman: The player who plays near third base. He is responsible for making an out by touching third base after he catches the ball before an opposing runner tries to touch third base. They also play defense around third base when the ball is hit.

Shortstop: The player who plays between second base and third base. They play defense in the area between second and third base when the ball is hit. They will also help the second baseman cover second base and make outs by touching second base when they have possession of the ball.

OutField: The right fielder, center fielder, and left fielder are three players that play in the outfield. They are responsible for catching fly balls as well as running down ground balls that make it through the infield. They then throw the ball into the infield to make outs and stop runs from being scored.

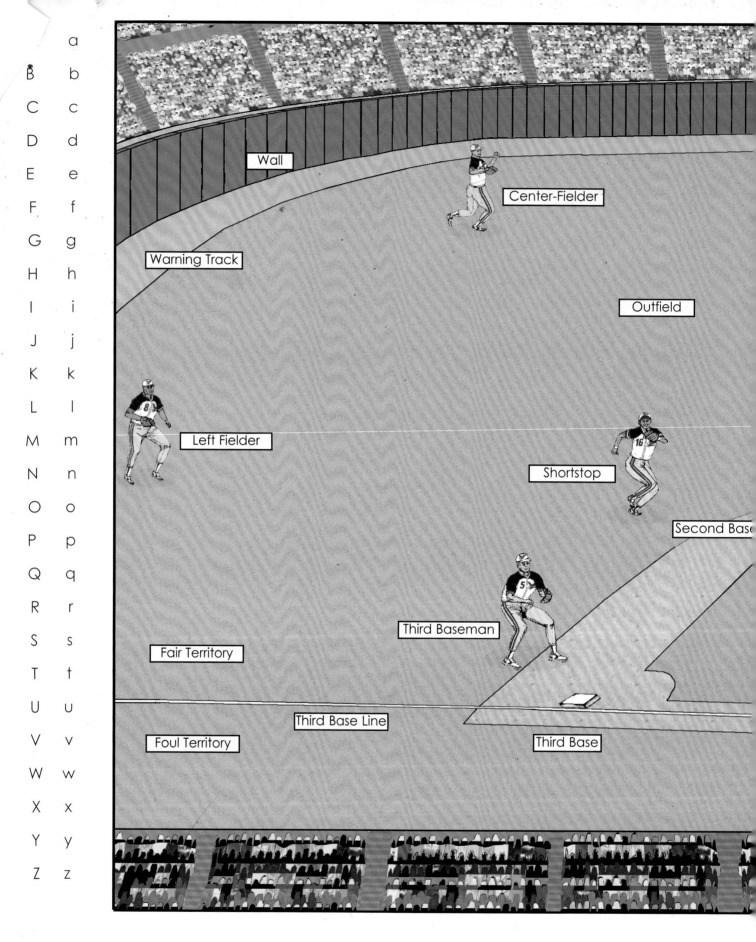

a
B b
C c
D d
E e
F f
G g
H h
I i
J j
K k
L l
M m
N n
O o
P p
Q q
R r
S s
T t
U u
V v
W w
X x
Y y
Z z

Wall

Center-Fielder

Warning Track

Outfield

Left Fielder

Shortstop

Second Base

Third Baseman

Fair Territory

Third Base Line

Foul Territory

Third Base

The Eagle fielders are all set as their pitcher takes aim.

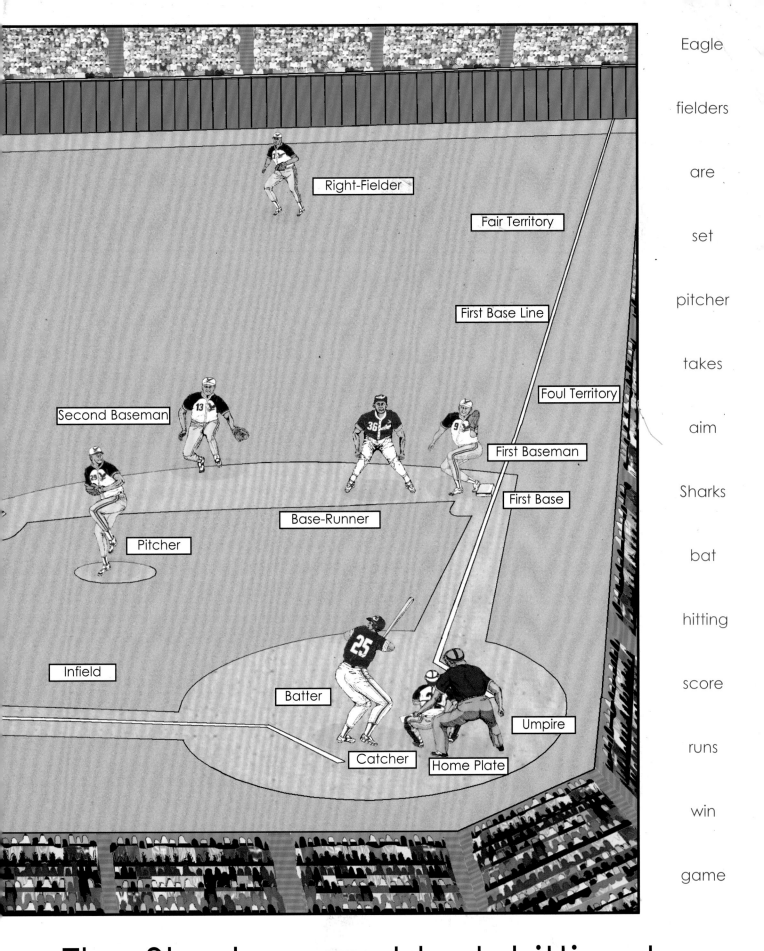

Right-Fielder

Fair Territory

First Base Line

Foul Territory

Second Baseman

First Baseman

First Base

Base-Runner

Pitcher

Infield

Batter

Umpire

Catcher

Home Plate

Eagle fielders are set pitcher takes aim Sharks bat hitting score runs win game

The Sharks are at bat, hitting to score runs and win the game.

Baseball Glossary

Ball: A pitch which does not pass through the strike zone and is not swung at by the batter (four balls thrown to a batter allows him to get on base).

Base: The four points of the baseball diamond, first, second and third bases and home plate. A base runner must touch each base in order to score a run.

Batter: The offensive player who is currently positioned in the batter's box set to hit the ball (hitter).

Batter's Box: The area on both sides of home plate where the batter stands during his time at bat.

Bottom: The last (second) half of an inning (example: bottom of the ninth inning).

Catch: When a fielder gains possession of the ball in his glove or hand before it touches the ground and firmly holds it.

Change-up: A pitch thrown by the pitcher at a slower rate of speed attempting to fool the hitter.

Curve Ball: A pitch thrown by the pitcher that will drop down or curve to one side; the pitcher is attempting to fool the hitter (they will swing where the ball will not be).

Defense: The team currently in the field.

Double: A play in which the batter runs and makes it safely to second base without stopping after hitting the ball.

Double Play: A defensive play in which two offensive players are put out as a result of one play of continuous action; the ball is caught and thrown between fielders and basemen.

Fast Ball: A pitch thrown very fast. The pitcher attempts to make the batter swing and miss the ball by overpowering the hitter with a very fast moving ball (brings in the heat).

Fielder: One of the nine defensive players in the field, including pitcher, catcher, first baseman, second baseman, third baseman, shortstop, left fielder, center fielder and right fielder.

Fly Ball: A ball which goes high in the air when batted (pop fly).

Foul Ball: A batted ball that lands on foul territory.

Ground Ball: A batted ball which rolls along the ground (grounder).

Home Plate: The base over which an offensive player bats, and to which he must return after touching all three bases in order to score a run. Where the pitcher aims each pitch and where the catcher plays his position.

Home Run: A play in which the batter makes it safely around all bases and back to home plate without stopping after hitting the ball.

Home Team: The team on whose field the game is played.

Infield: The diamond-shaped portion of the playing field bordered by the four bases.

Infielder: A fielder who plays in the infield, includes the pitcher, catcher, first baseman, second baseman, third baseman, and shortstop.

Inning: A period of time where both teams get a turn at bat while the other team plays defense. Each team is allowed three outs to try and score as many runs as they can each inning.

Line Drive: A ball which is batted directly to a fielder without touching the ground.

Offense: The team that is currently at bat trying to get hits and to score runs.

Out: A decision by the umpire that a player who is trying for a base is not entitled to that base. An out occurs when:
      1. A fly ball that is caught by a fielder.
      2. When the ball is thrown to a base before a player runs to that base.
      3. Three strikes have been called against a batter.

Outfield: The portion of the playing field that extends beyond the infield and is bordered by the first and third baselines.

Outfielder: A fielder who occupies a position in the outfield.

Pitch: When the ball is thrown by the pitcher to the batter (curve ball, fast ball, change-up).

Run: A score made when an offensive player (batter) has ran and touched all the bases and returned to home plate.

Runner: An offensive player who is advancing toward, touching or returning to any base (an offensive player on base).

Safe: A decision by the umpire that a runner who is trying for a base has not been tagged or forced out, and is therefore entitled to that base (is not out, is safe).

Single: A play in which the batter safely makes it to first base.

Strike: A pitch, which: 1. Is swung at by the batter and missed;
      2. Is not swung at, but the ball passes through the strike zone; (Umpire call)
      3. Is fouled by the batter when he has less than two strikes;
      (three strikes thrown to a batter and the batter is out)

Strike Zone: An area directly over home plate, from between the batter's knees to the area just below his chest (the umpire decides if a pitch is ruled a strike or a ball by using this zone).

Tag: The action of a fielder in touching a base with his body while holding the ball, or touching a runner with the ball, or with his hand or glove while holding the ball.

Throw: The act of propelling the ball toward another teammate. A pitch is not a throw.

Top: The first (beginning) half of an inning (example; the top of the ninth inning).

Triple: A play in which the batter makes it safely to third base without stopping.

Literacy Guide

Practice early reading skills using the special page format.

The special page format is designed to enhance the opportunity for children to practice key skills in their reading development. The chart below highlights 4 specific skills that are fundamental building blocks required to produce a new reader. Along with the story text in black at the bottom of each story scene there are letters in blue on the left and words in red on the right as a quick and handy reference to practice some of these skills.

Use their current ability as a guide to focus on the appropriate skills to practice.

4 Building Blocks Of Reading - With Suggested Reading Skills Activities

Oral Language Development

Speaking aloud and expressing ideas and thoughts builds oral language skills and provides an essential foundation for the development of reading.

Suggested Activities

- look through the story letting the child talk and tell about the pictures using their own words

- encourage, listen and actively respond to the child's own words, thoughts and ideas

- prompt for more oral discussion and detail with questions and rephrasing their words and ideas

- take turns talking about the action and what the players and fans might be feeling, thinking and saying

Letter and Sound Recognition

An essential pre-reading skill is recognizing all the letters (upper and lower case) of the alphabet and the sounds that they make.

Suggested Activities

- together point to each blue letter, name and make the sound of each letter in the alphabet

- explain letters have a lower case (small) symbol and upper case (big) symbol

- name a letter, the sound it makes and then have your child point to it (take turns making it a fun game)

- identify a letter and see if it can be found in a red word on the left and in the story (letters make words)

Building Word Vocabulary

An important reading skill development is the ability to visually identify words, to recognize the grouping of letters and to remember the word meaning.

Suggested Activities

- point to and say a red word, name each letter and their sounds that group together making each word

- point to and read a red word and then let your child find it in the story sentence (take turns making it a game)

- take turns pointing to and reading aloud each red word from the top to bottom in order

- point to a red word, have your child say the word and explain its meaning (make a sentence with the word)

Reading Fluency and Comprehension

Developing the ability to read words accurately and understand their meaning at the same time produces a fluent and competent reader.

Suggested Activities

- read the story together, develop a rhythm and use the rhyme to create and model a natural reading fluency

- ask questions about the action and events to check for memory and understanding

- discuss the thinking, emotions and feelings of the many players and spectators watching the game

- talk about team work, fair-play and sportsmanship, allowing your child to express their feelings and ideas

Find a good balance between working with your child's current abilities and challenging them to learn!

Please support the literacy development of your child.